(IM)PERFECT FATE OF MY PARAMOUR

DEVIL'S QUILL

Author's Note-

Im(perfect) Fate of Paramour, is my first fiction story. Every word I have put in this story is the product of my imagination & I had fun writing it.

The idea of writing this story came unexpectedly. I always wanted to write a fictional story but due to my college workload, I could not put all my efforts, though my mind was always filled with thoughts & ideas. This book exists because one morning as the sun was coming up. I decided by myself that I should pursue what I always wanted to do.

The story revolves around two lovers & their journey full of ups & downs, whether they will end up with each other or not, only time will tell.

Table of Contents-

Prologue-

In the heart of medieval India, a breathtaking tableau unfolds where the vibrant tapestries of daily life intertwine seamlessly with the ominous shadows of power struggles. Rising majestically against the vast azure sky, the magnificent Castle of Awadh stands as a testament to time, its formidable stone walls, weathered yet steadfast, reaching skyward like silent sentinels. They guard not only the regal treasures nestled within but also the rich, storied history of a land steeped in both grandeur and conflict. Enveloped by lush, rolling landscapes, fields of vibrant emerald stretch toward the horizon, swaying gently in the warm embrace of the breeze, painting a serene contrast against the turbulent tales that echo through the castle's imposing halls. Yet, beneath the majestic exterior of this grand fortress lies a realm fraught with palpable tension and unrest. The shadows of impending conflict loom ominously, with the air thick with the foreboding whispers of war that hang like a heavy mist. The relentless ambition of a rival Nawab casts a dark pall over the land, his ominous presence felt in every opulent courtly gathering and along every cobbled street where whispered conspiracies linger like clinging incense. Alliances once forged in trust now teeter precariously, hanging by the thinnest thread, as betrayal and distrust morph into unspoken truths. The hope for peace flickers like a fragile candle in the gathering storm, its light wavering against the encroaching darkness.

Amidst this backdrop of uncertainty and strife, a tender love story quietly begins to bloom, akin to a fragile blossom striving to thrive in a tumultuous garden. Radha, a spirited and devoted girl of only eleven, serves as the diligent assistant to the enchanting second princess of Maharaja

Yudhhamalla. Navigating the intricate web of court life with grace, Radha's agile mind races to balance the demanding expectations of her role while nurturing dreams that often feel tantalizingly distant. Despite the opulence that surrounds her, her heart finds its anchor in Vishnu, the brave and steadfast doorguard of the castle.

Their romance, wrapped in secrecy and nourished in the shadows of their shared childhood, flourishes like a delicate flower defiantly blooming amid the tempest. Radha and Vishnu, though separated by a vast chasm of social standing, have forged an unbreakable bond through fleeting moments of joy—stolen glances and hushed whispers that shatter the monotony of palace life. In the midst of lavish banquets and formal gatherings, their exchanges carry the weight of unexpressed emotions, each innocent smile and knowing look a testament to their hidden affection. For Radha, thoughts of Vishnu provide solace, his unwavering devotion resonating within the quiet chambers of her heart. To Vishnu, Radha embodies hope, her image a cherished treasure amid the chaos of their world.

As the seasons drift by, the initial spark of their affection intensifies, blossoming into a profound connection largely unnoticed by those around them. Each meeting teaches them to read the unspoken language woven between their hearts, a silent acknowledgment of feelings that grows stronger despite the constraints imposed by their societal roles. The court, with its strict hierarchy and watchful eyes, may erect barriers around them, but it cannot extinguish the fire ignited in their souls.

Then, on a fateful day thick with both hope and dread, the fragile tranquility of their existence is irrevocably altered. With a heart racing from a mix of intoxicating courage, swirling anxiety, and deep longing, Vishnu ventures to the secluded corners of the castle grounds where they once played carefree as children, their laughter ringing through the air like sweet music. The atmosphere hums with anticipation as he gathers his thoughts, swallowing hard against the tide of emotions threatening to overwhelm him.

With a voice trembling with sincerity, he confesses his deep affections, revealing how Radha has woven herself into the very fabric of his being. He paints her as the muse of his dreams, the radiant light brightening his darkest days, and dares to envision a world where the heavy burdens of duty and the looming shadows of war no longer weigh upon their hearts. In his eyes, one can see the fierce determination to protect her, to shield her from the encroaching chaos that threatens to unravel all the beauty they have discovered.

Yet, as their heartfelt declarations of love linger in the air like a fragile promise, they stand starkly contrasted by the harsh reality of their circumstances. Challenges abound, with the threats of conflict echoing ever closer as the kingdom teeters on the brink of war. Will the strength of their love withstand the trials that lie ahead, or will the relentless currents of fate sweep them apart, tearing them from their cherished dreams and leaving behind only the haunting echoes of what might have been? As their poignant story unfolds against a backdrop of turmoil and longing, one is left to ponder the timeless question: Do all love stories find their way to a joyous conclusion, or do some end with a wistful, bittersweet sigh, leaving echoes of lost potential lingering in the air?

Chapter 1:

The Untold Feelings

Trying is the first stage towards success,

A person who never tries always ends up regretting it.

Vishnu was consumed by a relentless yearning to unveil the depths of his profound affection for Radha, yet he found himself ensnared in a complicated web of circumstances. The absence of solitude—an essential backdrop for such delicate confessions—was constantly interrupted by the prying eyes of inquisitive courtiers, turning his meticulously planned declarations into a seemingly unattainable dream. He observed Radha as she moved with an ethereal grace through the adorned halls of the Castle, her very presence radiating an enchanting aura that captivated everyone in her vicinity. Her laughter, like a sweet melodic symphony, cascaded through the air, resonating off the elaborately embroidered tapestries and the glimmering chandeliers that graced the grand space. In her blissful state, she remained blissfully unaware of the tempest of emotions that raged within him, swirling like a storm yet to be released.

Despite his earnest endeavors to communicate his intentions—through fleeting glances laden with longing and moments of intimate proximity that crackled with unspoken tension—Radha perceived his peculiarities as mere endearing quirks of a devoted friend. The warmth of his gaze meant to convey a universe of feelings, went unnoticed, obscured beneath the layers of playful banter and camaraderie he maintained. Each day that passed sat heavily on his heart, as the burden of unexpressed love grew more oppressive. The reality of their relationship was harsh and inescapable; any dialogue with Radha risked scandal within the suffocating strictures of courtly decorum, dictated by the unyielding etiquette of their Kingdom. Such romantic overtures—viewed as unnecessary and utterly inappropriate—filled Vishnu with dread; the mere thought of a misstep overshadowed him, threatening dire repercussions, including possible banishment from the land he held dear.

Adding to his emotional turmoil was the ominous shadow of an impending war with the neighboring Nawab's territory. The atmosphere was thick with tension, palpable and foreboding, as soldiers honed their blades and strategists gathered in hushed tones, plotting in darkened corners. Vishnu's fate had become inextricably linked to that of his Kingdom, thrust into the esteemed yet daunting role of commander in one of the troops. This position demanded unquestionable respect and unwavering courage, making it all the more ironic that beneath his armor of responsibility, his heart writhed in agony beneath the weight of his concealed longing. With each tick of the clock, he sensed the opportunity to reveal his feelings to Radha slipping away like grains of sand through a sieve, leaving him trapped in a cycle of perpetual anguish.

In a moment ignited by desperation and a flicker of inspiration, Vishnu conceived a clever plan to encapsulate his fervent emotions within a secret letter—a strategy crafted to protect his true intentions from the watchful eyes roaming the castle corridors. He acquired a special liquid extracted from the vibrant yellow pulp of perfectly ripe lemons, renowned for its curious ability to vanish into obscurity when dry yet unveil its secrets under the gentle embrace of flame. With meticulous care, he dipped his brush into the citrus essence, lovingly etching his heartfelt sentiments onto a pristine sheet of parchment, his strokes both gentle and charged with a yearning that surged from deep within. Each word flowed like a whisper of his innermost hopes and fears, a raw revelation urgently seeking the light of day.

As he crafted his message, he clung to the intoxicating possibility that when the letter warmed against the flicker of a candle flame, the heat would awaken his hidden words, breathing life into the confession he had long held in check. In this delicate venture, shrouded in the shadows that enveloped the Castle and under the ever-looming threat of conflict, Vishnu cherished the hope that his carefully penned emotions would span the chasm that lay between them, illuminating a path directly to the core of his heart—a beacon daring to shine amidst the encroaching darkness.

He wrote-

"चकोर बहुत लंबे समय से चंद्रमा को देख रहा है, लेकिन यह हमेशा के लिए नहीं हो सकता है, क्या चंद्रमा वास्तव में इसके पास आ सकता है? इसे मेरी आखिरी इच्छा समझो, हम शायद इस युद्ध के बाद एक-दूसरे को कभी नहीं देख पाएंगे। क्या तुम मुझसे पूर्णिमा की रात नदी के पास मिल सकती हो ? "

He gently lobbed a folded letter through her open casement, its delicate parchment catching the warm evening breeze as it soared momentarily before gliding gracefully onto the cool stone floor of her chamber. The fading light of dusk enveloped him, casting an enchanting glow that embraced his figure, rendering him almost ethereal as he melted into the shadows. The deepening hues of twilight swirled around him, a cloak of anonymity heightened by the vibrant yet somber colors of the sky. Just beyond the window, the dense thickets of the Castle's Garden beckoned him like an uncharted haven of secrets, their allure tinged with the promise of mysteries yet to be revealed.

When Radha finally returned to her chamber after a long, taxing day laden with responsibilities and the weight of unspoken thoughts, she was met with an unexpected sight: the mysterious letter lay waiting for her, an enigma that sparked both intrigue and a flutter of trepidation within her. A wave of confusion swept over her brow as she picked up the letter; its surface was unblemished, an empty canvas devoid of words, yet vibrating with potential energy, like a still pond hiding the ripples of a stone yet to be cast.

Instinctively, she glanced outside, her gaze sweeping over the sprawling garden bathed in the soft, silvery glow of dusk. The rustling leaves whispered secrets to one another, carrying tales of the day's adventures, while the intoxicating scent of blooming jasmines and night-blooming flowers filled her senses with nostalgia and longing, but offered no clarity to unravel the riddle before her.

Just as she contemplated the possibility of discarding the seemingly unassuming piece of parchment, a glimmering reflection caught her eye, teasing her curiosity. Leaning closer, she noticed faint script, cleverly concealed among the folds, as if the letter itself was a treasure box waiting for her to carefully unearth its hidden secrets. Heart pounding with a mix of curiosity and wonder, Radha held the parchment over the flickering flames of her hearth. To her astonishment, the words began to emerge gradually, one by one, and she watched in disbelief as they revealed themselves in an elegant, flowing script, glowing softly against the backdrop of the fireplace.

The heartfelt missive, penned by Vishnu, unfolded before her like a gentle river winding through a lush landscape, each line coursing with a rhythm of longing and urgency. Every word resonated deep within her, stirring a torrent of emotions she thought long buried. As she drank in the final, poignant phrases—each syllable imbued with yearning—her heart raced, quickened by the thrill of anticipation, while a tight knot of trepidation twisted within her stomach. She found herself utterly captivated, lost in the eloquence of his expressions of love and devotion.

However, just as she savored the last words, the atmosphere in her chamber shifted abruptly. A sudden, frigid breeze swept in, heralding the entry of an unexpected intruder. A custodian, clad in a slate-gray uniform, stepped into her sanctuary with a disinterested expression that chilled her heart. The sound of his booted feet reverberated against the stone floor, breaking the intimate spell cast by Vishnu's letter. Radha's heart leaped into her throat, a primal instinct driving her to tuck the precious letter away in a flurry, hiding it beneath her skirts like a secret too precious to share.

Relief washed over her as the custodian casually mentioned that the Princess was inquiring about her whereabouts, revealing his oblivion to the significance of the letter she had just read, a blissful ignorance that felt like a small mercy. In a frantic moment of decision, she glanced back at the letter, and with a surge of desperation, tossed it into the hungry flames of the hearth. She watched, helpless yet resolute, as the flames eagerly licked at its corners, curling the edges and darkening the surface, devouring the words that had ignited her heart. A silent prayer for its secrecy slipped from her lips as she turned to exit the chamber, urgency propelling her feet toward the door, leaving behind a letter only partially singed, its edges still smoldering, clutching within it the memories of words that had set her soul ablaze.

Later that night, as shadows danced like phantoms in the flickering light of torch flames lining the ancient stone corridors of the castle, the custodian continued his rounds, the monotony of his duties a lullaby coaxing him to the brink of sleep. Yet, his keen gaze fell upon the partially charred letter that had escaped the flames, nestled precariously between the ancient stones of the hearth like a forgotten relic. A spike of suspicion pricked at his instincts; something about the parchment felt extraordinary, evoking a sense of intrigue far beyond its tattered appearance. His mind raced, convinced that this was no ordinary piece of paper but rather a potential relic of espionage or treachery. Without a second thought, he resolved to bring it to the attention of the Commander of the army, completely unaware of the storm of emotions and life-altering truths that lay hidden within the remnants of Radha's secret correspondence.

Chapter 2:
The Blissful Night Where They Unite

Nobody could see this world better

Then a man who is in Love.

The efforts he puts into another,

Sacrifices he makes,

How willingly he is trying to make

himself better.

On the eve of the full moon, a thrilling energy pulsed through the night air, enveloping the world in an enchanting shroud of mystery. Radha and Vishnu stood at the brink of an eagerly awaited reunion, their hearts brimming with anticipation. Above them, the moon radiated like a splendid sapphire, casting its silvery light down upon the velvety indigo sky. The moonlight danced upon the river's surface, creating a cascade of shimmering reflections that resembled a constellation of a thousand elusive stars, twinkling gently in the expansive canvas of night.

Vishnu had joyfully liberated himself from the weighty responsibilities of the day, embracing an exhilarating act of rebellion that allowed him to arrive early at their cherished secret meeting place along the riverbank. The sight before him was one that never ceased to evoke wonder. He nestled against the sturdy trunk of an ancient apple tree, its gnarled branches sprawling outward like welcoming arms, cradling him in their embrace. The melodic whispers of the river, serenading him like an old friend, enveloped him, each gentle ripple echoing the anticipation thrumming in his heart, harmonizing with the distant sounds of nocturnal creatures stirring to life under the soft moonlight.

As he settled into the familiar embrace of the night, his mind embarked on an exhilarating daydream, with each fantasy intricately more elaborate than the last. He envisioned a moment of pure bliss—a scene where he would find himself on one knee, a carefully chosen ring glistening between them, encapsulating the depth of his love in one precious object. Gradually, the tender words he longed to speak began to flow from his lips as effortlessly as the water sparkled beside him. He imagined them dancing gracefully beneath a soft blanket of moonlight, laughter intertwining with the evening breeze while the world around them faded into a blissful blur. This sacred moment would exist solely in each other's embrace, with the stars bearing witness to their silent vow. The warmth of this dreamy vision enveloped him, leading him to succumb to the hypnotic allure of the night and drift into a deep, peaceful slumber.

However, the serene hush of the night was soon pierced by a delicate sound—the soft jingle of an anklet that twinkled like distant stars, filling the air with an enchanting melody. A fragrant breeze wafted through, reminiscent of blooming white lilies releasing their sweet scent in a moonlit garden, each petal unfurling with grace and elegance. With a gentle flutter of his eyelashes, Vishnu awoke to behold a breathtaking figure standing before him. Radha, a vision of ethereal beauty, illuminated the darkness like the moon itself. Her mesmerizing blue eyes sparkled with a celestial luminescence, each glance brimming with warmth and vitality. Every delicate feature of her radiant face exuded an inner light that completely entranced him, rendering him momentarily speechless.

As she stood there, wrapped in a resplendent beige poshak that flowed around her like a gentle waterfall, Vishnu felt his heart race wildly in his chest. Her beauty was a breathtaking gift, a divine apparition that stole his breath away, suspending time itself as he remained lost in her allure. His adoration bubbled forth from deep within, and he could only whisper reverently,

"Hello?! Are you just going to stand there?" Radha teased playfully, her laughter ringing out like the soft tinkling of chimes, breaking the awkward silence that had encased them.

Finally shaking himself from the spell her beauty cast, Vishnu found his voice, stammering,

"You look so heavenly," his gaze fixed on her, utterly captivated by her enchantment. In a gesture of deep respect and overflowing

affection, he knelt before her, gently kissing her hand, cherishing the warmth that radiated between them and the undeniable magic of this moment.

A delicate shade of pink blossomed on Radha's cheeks as a soft smile graced her lips, each curve radiating joy and warmth.

"I've never seen a guard so charming before," she replied, her playful eyes dancing with mischief, igniting a spark of connection and light-heartedness between them.

As the moments unfurled and the moon slipped ever closer to midnight, the heavy weight of concern settled in Vishnu's chest.

"It's almost midnight; what took you so long to arrive?" he ventured, with dread thickening his voice, praying desperately that her tardiness had not endangered her safety.

Radha shifted slightly, the playful gleam in her eyes dimming as the harsh reality of their situation pressed down on her shoulders.

"It's very difficult for me to sneak out like this. I'm not supposed to be here, you know. If I get caught, I'll be in big trouble," she explained, her voice a mix of exhilaration and the heavy burden of their hidden love—a secret that shimmered in the dark yet loomed like an unseen shadow over them.

Together, they stood beneath the watchful gaze of the moon, a silent guardian to their heartfelt exchange—a tapestry woven from threads of longing and desire, binding two souls in a world that continually conspired to keep them apart. Each unspoken word hung delicately in the air, echoing their deep connection as they savored the fleeting moments of the night, fueled by a love that craved to flourish despite the constraints that surrounded them.

As their conversation unfolded, a profound sense of familiarity and connection blossomed between them, as if the fabric of their lives had intricately entwined despite this being their first direct encounter. Their bond, steeped in the essence of vivid childhood memories, was unmistakable. Radha had often found herself mesmerized as she stole glances at Vishnu during his spirited military training sessions. The sheer raw strength and unwavering discipline he exuded while executing his drills captivated her, each glimpse of him in his crisp uniform, glistening with sweat as he practiced with fierce focus, leaving an indelible impression upon her heart.

In return, Vishnu had once serenaded her under a starlit sky, his enchanting melodies flowing freely from his flute. The notes drifted softly through the balmy night air—like a secret echo of a dream wrapping around her as if it were a tender embrace. Now, fate seemed to playfully conspire as she insisted he perform again, her eyes sparkling with anticipation.

"How do you know that I play the flute?" he asked, a teasing smile curving across his lips, warm and inviting like the dawn breaking over a tranquil horizon.

"I know everything about you," she replied, laughter spilling from her lips like a gentle breeze rustling the leaves overhead, infusing the evening air with lightness.

"Now, enough with the questions; start playing for me! I want to hear those magical notes again!"

As twilight enveloped the surroundings, casting a dreamy veil over the landscape, Vishnu raised the flute to his lips, summoning ethereal notes that danced gracefully into the deepening night. The harmonious sound blended seamlessly with the soft rustle of the wind and the gentle lapping of water against the shore, creating a symphony of nature. Nearby, a nightingale, perhaps inspired by the sweet serenade, joined in, its song weaving a rich tapestry of sound that intertwined with their laughter, echoing their unique bond. They surrendered to a whimsical dance at the water's edge, a spinning celebration under the soft glow of the moon, their laughter ringing out like jubilant bells amidst the whispering secrets of the night.

As their dance slowed, yielding to a serene tranquility that only dusk can bring, Vishnu, ever the consummate gentleman, gracefully lifted Radha into a small, gently swaying boat. The surface of the water shimmered like a vast expanse of tiny stars, each ripple catching the light and reflecting it in a brilliant display of flickering diamonds. Once aboard, Radha's eyes sparkled with excitement, reminiscent of a starlit sky. She eagerly revealed a small container, delicately wrapped in soft cloth that radiated warmth and care—a tangible reflection of her deep affection.

"I made these for you," she announced, her voice bubbling with joy that infused the tranquil night air.

"Then you must feed me with your hands; I assure you that the taste of these sweets will be infinitely more delightful that way," he proposed, a gleam of mischief flickering in his eyes, challenging her with a playful spark. Radha chuckled, a light, joyous sound that danced around them.

"Alright, my brave soldier." With gentle fingers that moved with a dancer's grace, she selected one of the sweets and held it aloft to his lips, the delicate morsel taking on almost sacred importance at that moment. As he took a bite, the world around him faded into a surreal blur of colors and sounds. Then,

the unexpected realization that she had used salt instead of sugar struck him like a splash of cold water across his senses. Yet, despite the surprising flavor that now danced upon his tongue, he maintained an unwavering smile, an unyielding resolve to keep the moment light and joyful.

"So, how does it taste?" she asked, biting her lip in eager anticipation, her gaze locked onto him, her heart pounding with curiosity.

"Never tasted anything quite like this before," he admitted, his tone infused with playful curiosity, a hint of mischief sparkling in his eyes.

"So, is that a good thing or a bad thing?" she teased, her own eyes glinting with delight and a playful challenge.

"It's delicious," he replied, returning her gaze with a warm smile that melted away any lingering awkwardness, entwining them deeper in the enchanting fabric of their

shared moment. In that instant, beneath the luminous moonlit sky, they felt as if they were weaving a beautiful new memory, bound together by laughter, music, and the sweetness of unexpected flavors that lingered in the air.

Their laughter floated through the cool night air like a sweet, melodic tapestry, interwoven with threads of innocent joy that danced around them, casting a warm glow that eclipsed the minor culinary mishaps from earlier in the evening. Reclining on the gently rocking boat, the water enveloped them in a tender embrace, as if nature itself conspired to protect the intimacy of this extraordinary moment suspended in time.

"Close your eyes," he murmured softly, his voice a whisper in the tranquil silence that wrapped around them like a gentle, warm embrace, inviting her to surrender to the magic of the night.

"Why?" she asked, curiosity dancing in her tone, her eyes sparkling with intrigue amid the peaceful atmosphere that surrounded them.

"I have a special gift for you," he responded, anticipation threading through his words like golden light, transforming them into shimmering promises beneath the starry canopy above.

Radha, captivated by the earnestness in his voice, paused for a heartbeat before complying, her eyelids fluttering shut while a cascade of curious excitement bubbled within her, much like effervescent spring water bursting forth from the earth. With deliberate care, Vishnu reached into his pocket, his fingers brushing against the texture of a beautifully crafted ring. Adorned with sparkling stones that glinted like tiny constellations in the moonlight, it seemed to pulse with a life of its own. As he slid the exquisite piece onto her finger, he locked eyes with her, his gaze steady and sincere, revealing the depths of his soul. *"Would you like to spend the rest of your life with me?"* he asked earnestly, his words laced with hope and vulnerability.

"For me, you are my Queen," he continued, his voice rich and warm, each word resonating like a beloved melody in the stillness of the night air.

"Whenever I gaze upon you, all my worries and tensions simply vanish, replaced by a profound sense of peace that floods my heart." A warm, radiant rush surged through Radha at his heartfelt declaration, enveloping her like sunlight filtering through the dense canopy of a forest. Momentarily speechless, her heart raced like a wild river rushing through the valleys of her soul. In that exquisite instant, Vishnu leaned closer, enveloping her in his arms, drawing her gently toward him. She melted into his embrace, feeling the intoxicating

warmth of his presence surround her like a cozy blanket on a chilly night, cocooning her in safety and love.

"Now, whether I come back from the war or not, I will have no regrets," he whispered, each word imbued with deep emotion as if he were weaving a promise into the very fabric of their shared moment, a vow meant to withstand the trials of time.

"I will pray for your safety and prosperity during the war; nothing will harm you," she replied resolutely, her voice unwavering as she held him tighter, determined to chase away the shadows of uncertainty that lurked at the fringes of their intimate world.

"The moon is beautiful, isn't it?" Vishnu asked, his words carrying the weight of a profound sentiment, an unspoken vow of everlasting love that shimmered in the air like the sweet fragrance of blossoms in early spring.

"Yes, it truly is" she answered, her gaze lost in the bewitching glow of the moonlight, her heart swelling with affection and the warmth of hope.

Embracing the magical atmosphere that cloaked them, Vishnu revealed a mesmerizing red ruby ring from the folds of his cloak, its facets shimmering like distant stars against the velvety backdrop of the night sky.

"Will you share your life with me?" he asked once more, his voice thick with emotion, hinting at the weight of a life-altering decision.

Just as they leaned in, poised to seal their promise with a tentative, breathless kiss, their serene, enchanted moment was suddenly shattered. Without warning, a sudden attack surged from the shadows—an ominous flaming arrow sliced through the night air with alarming speed, striking their boat with a violent explosion. In the blink of an eye, tranquility metamorphosed into chaos, transforming their world into a frantic struggle for survival amid the flickering remnants of their precious, stolen moment.

Chapter 3:
The Harsh Dawn

Acceptance of the fact that life

Never go as planned,

But that's the thing with humans,

They will never stop planning.

The tranquil evening transformed into a nightmarish experience as the small boat they were on became engulfed in flames, a consequence of the soldiers carrying out the orders of the Commander-in-chief. In a frantic bid for survival, Radha and Vishnu were forced to plunge into the frigid waters. Upon reaching the river bank, they found themselves encircled by soldiers. The attendant who had been accompanying them then revealed the letter he had stumbled upon in Radha's quarters.

"You have done well, gatekeeper! You have apprehended her!" Commander-in-Chief says.

"Arrest her! She's a spy!" bellowed the Commander-in-chief.

Paralyzed with fear, Radha watched as a soldier advanced to seize her. In a courageous attempt to rescue her, Vishnu exclaimed, *"It was me! I penned that letter!"*

The Commander in Chief interrogated, *"What do you mean?"*

"Yes! I wrote that letter. I was composing it for someone else, but she inadvertently received it. I tried to escape, but she caught me on that boat," explained Vishnu.

"Are you a spy then?" inquired the Commander-in-chief.

"No! I would never betray my homeland," protested Vishnu." That will be determined by the jury.

"Soldiers, arrest him," ordered the Commander-in-chief.

As the soldiers moved to seize Vishnu, Radha knelt and pleaded with the Commander-in-Chief to spare him. Gazing into Radha's eyes, Vishnu smiled and whispered, *"We will meet again and be together forever."*

Radha, with tears streaming down her face, made a solemn vow amidst her anguish,

"I will endure the passage of time, waiting for you, even if it takes another lifetime."

Vishnu found himself ensnared in the stifling gloom of a dimly lit cell, an enveloping darkness that felt almost suffocating, wrapping around him like an oppressive shroud. The air was thick with a palpable despair, clinging to his skin and weighing down his spirit. The cold stone walls, rough and unforgiving, loomed around him, their surfaces textured like the pain etched into his heart. Each murmur of wind echoed within the confines of his prison, amplifying the anguish that reverberated through his very being, creating a haunting symphony of sorrow that resonated deep within his core. The faint flicker of a solitary torch cast erratic shadows that danced across the damp stone, whispering cruel reminders of the freedom that now felt like an unreachable dream, glimmering just beyond the oppressive veil of darkness.

The soldiers, grim specters of authority, had wrenched him from a life that had once felt serene and secure, unceremoniously thrusting him into this bleak existence. Hope had not merely faded into the backdrop; it had become an alien concept, a shimmering mirage in the arid wasteland of his despair. As he wrestled with the tumultuous storm of emotions surging within him—fear gnawing insidiously at the edges of his sanity, regret festering like an untreated wound that throbbed with every heartbeat, and sorrow anchoring him in despair—he retreated to the farthest corner of his confines. There, shrouded in shadows that flickered ominously around him, he stumbled upon another lost soul, a fellow inmate whose gaunt visage bore the marks of suffering. This stranger's eyes sparkled with a blend of curiosity and deep empathy as if silently urging Vishnu to share his burden.

"You seem to hail from a distinguished background," the inquisitive inmate remarked, breaking the oppressive silence that enshrouded them like a dense fog. His voice emerged low yet clear, slicing through the heavy atmosphere and evoking a spark of connection amid their shared torment.

"What series of events led to your unjust confinement within these cursed walls? What calamities conspired to entrap you in

this place of sorrow?" His question hung in the stale air, weighted with sincerity and a fierce hunger to comprehend the shared plight of those bound by the chains of their circumstances.

With a heavy heart, Vishnu prepared to unravel the painful tapestry of his past, each thread woven with heartbreak.

"I succumbed to love," he began, his voice trembling as it emerged from the depths of his soul, imbued with profound remorse and aching longing.

"In that intoxicating moment of passion, I believed that I could transcend the invisible barriers erected by society, that love could serve as a mighty force capable of rewriting our destinies. Yet, here I stand, ensnared within these merciless walls, faced with the brutal reality that life is far from the idyllic fairy tale I once cherished. Those enchanting stories, rich with the promise of unending joy, are crafted for the fortunate

few—those who revel in palaces, not for someone like me, whose spirit now lies shackled, imprisoned not merely by these stones, but by the very act of daring to love."

He paused, a mountainous weight of anguish building in his chest, as hot tears streamed down his face, cascading onto the cold, unyielding ground like raindrops falling upon the parched earth. Each drop felt like a shard of his soul, a reminder of extinguished dreams and lost potential.

"How could I have been so selfish?" he murmured, his voice cracking beneath the immense weight of self-reproach as if his own sorrow had taken on a life of its own and was pressing down on him.

"In my reckless pursuit of happiness, I have wrought ruin not just upon myself but upon her as well. It was a delicate dream, once vibrant and full of life, now reduced to mere ash, a haunting specter of what could have

been. And now, I must endure the relentless consequences of my choices."

As he spoke, a visceral sense of despair settled in the stagnant air, intertwining his fate irrevocably with that of his fellow prisoner in misery. It forged an unspoken bond amid their shared suffering, a haunting connection that bridged their pain. The shadows around them deepened, as if the darkness itself bore witness to their tales of lost hope, forever etching their despair into the very stone walls that confined them, leaving an indelible mark on the world around them.

"As I sit here, enveloped in a cocoon of nostalgia, a tempest of memories swirls around me, much like an emotional tide surging onto the shores of my heart. This reminiscence intertwines with the bittersweet narrative of unrequited love that colored my youth in vibrant hues, each shade swirling vividly in the tapestry of my

mind. The object of my unwavering affection was none other than the farmer's daughter, an ethereal beauty whose flowing hair flowed like strands of sunlit wheat, dancing gracefully in the soft caress of the breeze, shimmering warmly beneath the unrelenting brilliance of the summer sun. Her eyes sparkled with a rich cerulean that mirrored the endless expanse of the azure sky above, radiating an aura of wonder and joy that felt almost otherwordly. Her laughter, a melodious chiming imbued with innocence and mirth, rang out across the sun-drenched fields, frolicking playfully with the wind and drawing me ever closer as if I were a moth irresistibly drawn to a flickering flame."

"There were days when I would wander along the dusty, sun-bleached paths of our quaint little town, my heart racing with eager anticipation at each step. I would traverse 5 to 10 kilometers, each stride fueled by the hope of catching a fleeting glimpse of her as she toiled beneath the

unyielding sun, side by side with her father, amidst the sprawling landscapes of golden grain, or as she strolled toward the village with her lithe frame, cradling baskets overflowing with the day's fresh harvest. Every stolen glance at her felt akin to unearthing a hidden treasure, igniting a warm spark within me that swirled with exhilaration and longing, a medley of emotions that lingered like the sweet fragrance of ripened fruit wafting through the summer air."

"Then, on a fateful afternoon etched in my memory, I found myself concealed behind a dense cluster of trees, eagerly observing the scene unfold before my eyes. My heart raced with excitement until, with an unfortunate crack, the snapping of a twig shattered the delicate silence of the moment. To my utter horror, she turned, her gaze piercing through the leafy curtain and capturing my

startled eyes in a moment frozen in time. Panic surged through my veins, scripting an impulsive retreat in my mind, but my legs betrayed me, locking in place as if enthralled by a spell. With hesitant steps, she approached, a curious smile unfurling on her lips, casting a soft, warm glow akin to the blush of twilight across her cheeks. In that fleeting instant, my heart raced—each thump reverberated with the thudding anxiety of the moment, echoing loudly in my ears."

"Instead of the anticipated anger or disdain, her features softened, illuminated by a kindness that caught me off guard. With a gentle warmth in her voice, she offered me a simple farewell—an exchange that held an unspoken understanding flickering like a fragile spark between us. Little did I know that this serendipitous encounter would weave itself into the very fabric of my life.

As days transformed into weeks, we found ourselves inexplicably drawn to one another, as if guided by a force beyond our comprehension. We spent countless hours beneath the vast expanse of the sky, our laughter resonating like sweet music through the tranquil air, weaving secrets and dreams among the whispering leaves of the old oak trees, timeless sentinels that bore witness to our budding connection."

"Every moment shared felt like stepping into a fantastical realm, infused with magic all its own. When twilight descended, the golden hues of the sunset enveloped everything in a soft, ethereal glow, filling my heart with a bittersweet cocktail of gratitude entwined with longing—an intoxicating blend of burgeoning love, woven tightly with the poignant ache of yearning for something that always seemed to flutter just beyond my grasp."

"Some days later, I heard a loud noise coming from her cottage. I found out that the soldier had brutally killed her father and they were trying to abduct her. I saw one of the soldiers grab her by the Hair and throw her to the ground. She resisted, but it wasn't enough. I managed to gather the courage to throw a stone at one of the soldiers, hitting his head. Another soldier came towards me and wounded me with his sword."

"They took the girl deep into the forest. I pursued their trail and when I caught up to them, I found out that the girl had marks and scratches all over her body & she was brutally raped by the soldiers, I Remember this story vividly: they thought she was dead and left her in the bushes to be eaten by a wild animal."

"I remember that moment as if it were etched in my mind. It was a dark and stormy night, the kind that sends shivers down your spine. The rain poured heavily, and the wind

howled through the trees, creating an almost eerie atmosphere. I moved quickly, my heart pounding in my chest as I scooped her up, fearing she was unconscious and in desperate need of help. Just as I was about to rush her to safety, she suddenly stirred, her eyes flickering open. In a soft yet urgent voice, she called out to me, 'Pihu!' – the affectionate nickname she always used that made my heart swell."

"In that precarious moment, she poured her heart out to me. She shared her feelings, her love for me that had blossomed over our time together. It was a bittersweet confession, filled with both sweetness and sorrow. Even in the face of her tragic fate, she looked at me with such warmth and strength, reassuring me that she would always be by my side, even if the world around us crumbled."

"Regrettably, my memories are now tainted by the knowledge that I couldn't give her the

farewell she truly deserved. The soldiers had come, merciless and indifferent, intercepting us as we sought refuge. They took her away, disposing of her body as if she were a discarded object, stripping away my chance to honor her life with a proper burial. A decade has passed since that fateful night, but the pain remains a constant companion, a reminder of what was lost. I feel an unwavering resolve growing within me— once I am finally free, I will search for her remains. I need to give her the peaceful rest she was robbed of."

As Vishnu spoke with another inmate, He found common ground in his shared longing for closure. He, too, expressed a deep desire to honor those he had lost, echoing his sentiment about the importance of a respectful farewell. It was a moment of connection. With empathy in his voice, He acknowledged his pain, reminding him that every individual has a purpose that must be fulfilled before leaving this world.

They both understood that acknowledging thier losses is essential and as they bid each other goodbye, Vishnu felt a flicker of hope—maybe, just maybe, we could both find peace in our quests for remembrance.

Chapter 4:

Is This What The Fate Has Decided?

Sometimes life has its way to test you,

It has its way of teaching you a lesson.

But hey! There is no fun in success without failure & sacrifices.

In the shadowy, damp confines of the prison, an oppressive atmosphere of despair clung to every corner, thick enough to suffocate the spirit. The air, heavy with the stench of mildew and neglect, seemed to absorb the sorrow of countless forgotten souls. Vishnu reclined in his cramped cell, the flickering light of a solitary candle casting ghostly silhouettes that danced erratically across the cold, unyielding stone walls, as if the very shadows mirrored his tumultuous emotions. The feeble flame, wavering like his hope, illuminated the contours of his anguished face—once a beacon of warmth—now etched with lines of despair. His heart, once buoyant with dreams of a joyful reunion with his beloved Radha, now felt like a lead weight, dragging him deeper into the abyss of uncertainty with each agonizing second that slipped by. Outside these grim walls, Radha's once-radiant health had taken a precipitous turn; the vibrant spirit that had always lit up her world now flickered weakly, smothered by the heavy suffocation of sorrow and isolation that draped over her like a shroud.

As the fateful day loomed closer—when the Awadh kingdom's army would march into a battle against the formidable Nawab—Radha sat in her opulent chamber, her elegance standing in stark contrast to the storm brewing within her. The exquisite details of her surroundings—from the intricately gilded carvings that adorned her sumptuous furniture to the rich, flowing silks enveloping her canopy bed—only amplified the turmoil churning inside her heart. Her once bright eyes, usually sparkling like the finest jewels, now appeared dull and distant, her gaze fixed vacantly on the window. The tranquil river outside, lazily meandering beneath a pale sky, served as a haunting reminder of the peaceful days spent with Vishnu beside its banks, sharing laughter and weaving dreams of a bright future together. Waves of nostalgia washed over her, saturating her spirit with bittersweet memories of joy, whispered hopes, and warm embraces. But as the threat of war loomed ever closer, those cherished recollections twisted into melancholic reminders of everything that could be irrevocably lost, amplifying her profound longing for Vishnu and igniting a flicker of hope for their eventual reunion.

Suddenly, the eerie stillness enveloping the castle was violently shattered by a thunderous explosion that reverberated through the air, the deep rumble mingling with the deafening splintering crash of a cannonball crashing into the sturdy outer wall. The cacophony of shattering wood and anguished cries erupted simultaneously, transforming a day that had begun with a fragile sense of calm into one of destruction and terror. The serene atmosphere was instantly swallowed by chaos; panic-stricken servants screamed and scattered in every direction, while the defenders of Awadh steeled themselves, the grim reality of battle dawning upon them as they braced against the onslaught.

The merciless soldiers of the Nawab's army surged into the castle like a dark tide, their battle cries echoing ominously against the grand stone walls. The steadfast defenders of Awadh met the brutal intrusion with resolute determination, their faces hardened by the weight of impending conflict. A palpable tension, thick as fog, wrapped around them as soldiers exchanged steely glances, fully aware of the formidable odds they faced. From the towering Castle's Dome, a clarion call for unity and courage rang out—a trumpet blast cutting through the din like a beacon of hope, urging the brave warriors to fight not only for their homeland but for their loved ones and their very existence.

Amidst the tumult, a sense of urgency wrapped the castle like an oppressive shroud; guards were hastily summoned, their heavy boots echoing on the stone floor as they rushed to confront the encroaching invaders. The clash of swords, mingled with cries of battle, filled the air, drowning out all remnants of tranquility. Yet, amidst this frenzy, fate intervened with a shocking flourish. In the chaos, a guard's grip faltered, and the heavy ring of keys clattered to the floor with a resounding crash—each key striking the ground with an echo that seemed to freeze time for a heartbeat. Just then, a diminutive mouse scurried into view, its tiny, nimble body darting through the chaos with unexpected agility. In the blink of an eye, it seized one of the keys, clutching it firmly between its small teeth and scurrying off toward Vishnu's cell, a glimmer of hope amidst the despair.

Overcome by a rush of gratitude and a tingle of anticipation, Vishnu recognized the golden opportunity that lay before him. As the little creature dropped the key with perfect precision at the foot of his cell door, desperation surged through him. With one swift, determined motion, he turned the key in the lock, the rusty hinges groaning in protest as he stepped into the corridor. The air was thick with the acrid scent of smoke, mingling with the palpable tension of imminent danger. In a bold act of camaraderie, he hurriedly liberated Pihu, his fellow inmate, just as the ominous chorus of approaching enemies swelled in the distance. The two exchanged a glance brimming with unspoken understanding and fierce resolve.

Meanwhile, in her chamber, Radha had secured the door to her lavish quarters, but anxiety gnawed at her insides, relentless and sharp. She pressed her trembling palms against the ornately barred window, her heart pounding in her chest as she caught sight of Vishnu emerging into the fray, a flicker of determination illuminating his features amidst the encroaching chaos.

"She is my beloved!" Vishnu exclaimed, his voice echoing across the landscape, infused with fervent hope and unyielding determination. The air around him buzzed with anticipation as he gazed towards the horizon, where the sun plunged low, spilling a cascade of golden light over the land like liquid gold. The thought of seeing her again, after an eternity apart, felt almost like a distant dream—a surreal possibility he dared to embrace. An unexpected twist of fate had revealed a path he had long believed lost to him, and he understood he couldn't allow this precious opportunity to slip through his fingers.

"I will do whatever it takes to rescue her," he vowed, his heart pounding fiercely as he solidified his resolve.

Standing beside him, Pihu radiated an aura of fierce determination, her eyes shimmering with a light that mirrored his own passion. *"You're risking everything by going alone!"* she exclaimed her voice a steady yet urgent plea that cut through the evening stillness.

"I can't just stand idly by and watch you embark on this perilous journey without offering my help. I will not let you face this challenge by yourself; I'm coming with you," she insisted, a fierce spark igniting in her gaze as if she were a flame ready to blaze brightly against the encroaching darkness.

Vishnu turned to her, worry etching his brow as he searched her eyes for insight. *"But why would you put yourself in harm's way for me?"* he questioned, genuine puzzlement softening the lines of his face. He admired her bravery, yet he couldn't fathom the depths of her selflessness, the willingness to jeopardize her own safety for someone else's dream.

Pihu's expression softened, revealing her compassion like a flower unfurling its petals to the sun. *"Though my own love story may forever remain a dream, I recognize the immeasurable weight this quest holds for you & you might think that I am a little crazy but I don't think that you got those cell keys out of luck, it can't be a mere coincidence. I think it's my girl spirit & she wants me to help you,"* he replied, his voice tender yet resolute.

"Fate has blessed you with a flicker of hope, and it would be an honor to stand by your side, aiding you in reuniting with your beloved. So tell me, are you truly prepared for this treacherous mission? It will not be easy, and I may very well become your shield against whatever formidable challenges lie ahead!"

A surge of gratitude washed over Vishnu as he regarded his steadfast friend, her unwavering support enveloping him like a warm embrace.

"Thank you so much, my dear friend. Your willingness to stand beside me means more than words can convey," he expressed, feeling the bond of resilience forged a powerful connection between them. In that moment, he knew he would not face this daunting journey alone; they would confront the unknown together, as allies against the trials that awaited.

Vishnu and Pihu entered the castle from the secret passage, when they were entering the Main Hall they saw that the place was filled with dead bodies, & blood was scattered everywhere.

Radha on the other hand hides in the closet and locks it from inside. Vishnu & Pihu quickly reached her room, they pushed the door but it was locked from the inside.

'Take this' Pihu gave a hairclip which he was keeping with him as the last memory of his Lover to Vishnu & asked him to pick the lock. Vishnu was trying desperately to open

the lock. Suddenly, an arrow from the opposite side of the path was shot at him by one of the soldiers who saw them but Pihu pushed Vishnu aside and took the arrow at himself, The arrow hit straight into his throat silting it in half. A Series of arrows were shot at Vishnu but Pihu took it all over him, he made himself the shield for

Vishnu. The soldier ran out of the arrow so he drew his sword and ran to kill Vishnu, Pihu was lying on the floor taking his last breathes he pretended as if he was already dead, the soldier told Vishnu to get on his knees and put his hand behind his back. Vishnu does exactly what the soldier told him to do.

While the soldier was tying his hands, Pihu gathered all the strength that possessed him pulled one arrow out of his body, and shoved it into the soldier's forehead killing him instantly.

'*Why did you do that, my friend?*' Vishnu cried.

Pihu's gentle gazed at him & said-

"*I vowed to shield you, and now my purpose is served, my dear boy. I sense my love patiently awaiting my arrival. The time has come for us to reunite. You will find your beloved in this earthly realm, while mine awaits me beyond. I can see her. Farewell, my dear boy.*"

With those poignant words, Pihu drew his final breath, and his soul gracefully departed from his earthly vessel, joining his beloved. Meanwhile, as Vishnu approached the door, he envisioned himself and Radha fleeing the castle, leaving the kingdom behind, and embarking on a tranquil life together.

He clung to the belief that all the waiting and sacrifices would prove worthwhile. However, as he turned the doorknob, a wave of numbness engulfed his body.

The room lay bare, and his heart skipped a beat. The only thought he had was that either Radha was brutally killed by the enemies or she had left the castle without him. A group of enemy soldiers approached him, and he had no choice but to jump out of the window into the pond full of crocodiles.

Radha, on the other hand, fell unconscious in the closet because her health condition was already deteriorating. The soldiers locked her room from outside when they found nobody in the castle.

She had no strength to move her body and get out of the closet. She spends 4 days in the closet as she awaits her death in the dark, the air gets thick. Suddenly, she heard the sound of mice. She realized that she was not the only one awaiting her demise. Her body starts to become lifeless as mice start to feed soul out of her body and she surrenders herself, waiting for Vishnu to save him.

Chapter 5:
Life After War

Cries of the war are heard by only those,

Who lost their loved one in it.

The Nawab's Soldiers captured the Castle of Awadh, and all the important Commanders who survived the war were put in solitary confinement and tortured by experimenting on their body making them vulnerable to disease to see how a human body responds to it. Some of them were made food tasters. The king was forced to be intoxicated various drugs were administered to him to make a living dead object.

More than half of Queens and Princesses committed Johar (the deliberate act of setting oneself in the holy flame, a practice followed by women, so that the enemy couldn't exploit them and their body). Those who did not gather enough courage were made sex slaves by the Nawab's soldiers.

The mortal remains of Radha were still waiting for someone to give her the funeral she deserved. Soul was stuck in a loop and she was in pain. She had a feeling that the person who loved her the most had betrayed her. Her spirit was under the control of her anger. Radha's room had been locked and had never been opened since the soldiers locked it.

Vishnu, on the other hand, was last seen jumping into a river teeming with crocodiles. The soldiers pursued him but couldn't trace him, and the chances of him coming out alive were next to impossible.

Nawab undertook the ambitious task of conducting a thorough survey of the treasure. This involved creating a detailed map that revealed the intricate network of hidden passageways within the castle, leading to a vast collection of gold coins, precious stones, and jewelry. The map was meticulously crafted, with intricate details that posed a challenge even to the most experienced treasure hunters. Nawab called upon all the skilled treasure hunters in his domain to unravel the secrets hidden within the castle. Despite their numerous attempts and diverse strategies, the treasure hunters found themselves repeatedly facing insurmountable obstacles. Out of frustration, the Nawab ordered them to be hanged in public, considering them a disgrace to their profession. Now, the Nawab knows that if there is any treasure in this castle, only one person could find it.

Chapter 6:
The Adventurous Fella

Putting oneself in danger by putting food on the table,

To give life to your family you never had,

The compromise one makes to fulfill their child's desire,

Is another form of love.

At Ennore Port in Madras, the lively symphony of the harbor began to fade as the sun slowly descended toward the horizon, casting a breathtaking array of vibrant oranges, deep purples, and soft pinks across the sky—a dazzling canvas that echoed the tumultuous emotions swirling within Saanvi. She stood solitary on the old wooden docks, the planks twisted and sun-bleached from years of relentless salt and sunlight, feeling as if the very weight of her heart was pressing hard against her ribcage. Before her, her beloved Avyaan readied himself for yet another dangerous treasure hunt, each step he took away from her intensifying the sense of dread coiling in her stomach.

"Promise me, Avyaan! This is the last time you go on a treasure hunt. After this, please, no more risking your life," she implored, her voice quivering with a potent mix of love and anxiety, intertwining like delicate vines in a wild garden. Her eyes sparkled like the luminous evening star, brimming with a depth of concern that words could never fully articulate—the relentless worry that had shadowed her every moment since he first embarked on these reckless quests.

Avyaan paused, turning to her, his face illuminated by the waning daylight, which cast a soft glow upon him. He offered her a tender smile, a gesture meant to soothe her fears.

"I promise, my love. I'm so close to uncovering the legendary treasure hidden on Catchall Island in the Bay of Bengal. Just imagine! Once I find it, we can leave behind all our struggles—the sleepless nights, the empty pockets—and embrace a life overflowing with comfort and joy." His voice resonated with an unwavering determination, painting a vivid picture of hope and possibility, and the excitement shimmering in his eyes sparkled like the sun-drenched waves kissing the shore.

"You are my treasure," Saanvi declared, desperation lacing her words as she tightened her grip around his arm, an anchor trying to tether him to the safety of their present moment.

"I don't need jewels or gold. As long as I have you, I am content." Wrapping her arms around him, she held him close, her heart

pounding as if wanting to shield him from the lurking unknown that awaited him in the depths of his quest. Avyaan felt the warmth of her embrace seep deeply into his soul, momentarily washing away the surge of adrenaline surging through him at the thought of adventure. Yet, as he inhaled the familiar scent of her hair—a mix of jasmine and the salty breeze—a bittersweet realization gnawed at his heart, threatening to spill over into tears he fought to contain.

"You are my greatest treasure," he whispered back, his voice thick with emotion as he reciprocated her embrace, drawing her close as if to memorize every detail of the moment—a sensation so profound that he felt it engraving itself into the very fabric of his soul. He understood in that fleeting instant that he would carry this fragment of her essence with him into the vast, unknown expanse that lay ahead.

As the dawn's first light began to peek over the horizon, casting a warm glow that danced upon the water, turning it into a shimmering canvas of silvery hues, Avyaan reluctantly pulled away from her comforting presence. He stepped back, bidding her a heartfelt farewell, the weight of their shared moments heavy on his heart. His silhouette slowly merged with the awakening world around him, dissipating into the embrace of uncertainty as he ventured forth in pursuit of the legendary golden relic that had eluded countless adventurers before him.

Seven grueling days passed, marked by relentless toil and testing his physical limits. He battled insistent fatigue that clung to him like a shadow, endured the scorching heat that beat upon him mercilessly and contended with the untamed elements of nature that seemed to conspire against his quest. Finally, he set foot on the rugged terrain of Catchall Island, its wildness both daunting and invigorating. The air was thick with humidity, wrapping around him like a heavy shroud, while dense foliage loomed ominously, creating an eerie silence that amplified his exhaustion and feelings of isolation.

He paused for a brief moment, allowing the salty breeze to wash over his sunburned skin, momentarily easing the discomfort that clung to him. However, the call of the treasure pushed him forward, and he soon resumed his frantic search, scouring the island for any indication of the fabled golden relic. With fingers digging through the dense underbrush and feet scaling the jagged, rocky outcrops, he poured every ounce of energy into his efforts. Yet, after countless hours of labor, not a single clue seemed to surface, and frustration began to gnaw at the edges of his resolve, a persistent hunger-like ache that seemed to threaten his mission and dampen his spirit.

That night, beneath a vast expanse of stars twinkling like distant diamonds scattered across a velvety sky, Avyaan sank wearily against the gnarled roots of a towering tree, the weight of his mounting disappointment wrapping around him like an oppressive fog. Doubt seeped into his mind, lurking like a specter and sowing seeds of uncertainty as he questioned his abilities and the choices he had made that led him to this desolate island. The eerie stillness of the surroundings felt mocking, its only sound was the distant roar of the restless sea crashing against the rocky shore.

In that unsettling silence, a forlorn figure materialized from the shadows—an emaciated dog with disheveled fur, whose once-vibrant eyes now appeared dulled by the heavy burden of loneliness and despair. The dog approached cautiously, each tentative step a testament to its flickering hope and resilience in the face of abandonment, its frame quivering as it navigated the darkness.

As Avyaan crouched down, he felt an overwhelming rush of empathy wash over him at the sight of the dog's worn collar—an unspoken symbol of a loyal companion who had once roamed the island freely. The sight stirred something deep within him, and he instinctively reached out, his hand extending toward the fragile creature. The dog responded with gentle whimpers, its eyes shimmering with unshed tears, communicating its longing for connection and companionship in a world that had turned its back on it.

Moved profoundly by the plight of this abandoned creature, Avyaan knelt beside it, using the limited supplies he had. With careful hands, he tended to the dog's wounds, trying to soothe the pain and discomfort that had etched themselves onto its body. He shared the scant remnants of his provisions—meager pieces of dried fish and a few bites of bread—creating an unspoken bond that transcended words between them.

Gradually, under the warmth of his touch and the kindness of his actions, the dog's spirit began to reignite. A flicker of hope blossomed amidst the desolation that surrounded them, igniting a shared resilience in both their hearts. In that vulnerable moment, as they found solace and strength in one another's company, Avyaan realized that he had stumbled upon an unexpected treasure of his own—a burgeoning friendship born from shared struggle, empathy, and compassion that would forever change the course of his journey.

As the sun began its graceful descent beneath the horizon, the sky transformed into a breathtaking canvas, splashed with vivid strokes of fiery orange and soft, delicate pink. These warm hues gradually melted into one another, giving way to the deepening, velvety blues of the encroaching night, as if the universe itself were preparing for a tranquil slumber. Avyaan approached the tranquil shoreline with a sense of solemn purpose, his heart swelling with anticipation as he sought to carve out his own little sanctuary amidst the evening's embrace.

With careful deliberation, he unpacked his selection of supplies, each item harboring memories of past escapades—the sturdy tent, his sleeping bag, and a hand-carved walking stick, all whispering stories of adventures shared and challenges overcome. As he assembled his refuge, the sound of the waves rhythmically kissing the shore provided a calming backdrop, mingling with the gentle rustle of leaves overhead. The cool breeze brushed against his skin, invigorating him as he set to work, and soon the crackling fire he tended began to blaze brilliantly. Flames leaped and danced, twisting and swirling in the night air, their warm glow flickering against the backdrop of the darkening sky, casting playful shadows that danced across the golden grains of sand.

The light enveloped him in a comforting embrace, creating an oasis of warmth that contrasted beautifully with the encroaching chill of the evening. Nearby, his loyal dog, a faithful companion with soulful eyes, curled up against him, radiating a warmth that transcended the physical. Its soft fur provided gentle support, becoming a vigilant guardian in the tranquil stillness of the moonlit night. Together, they formed a serene tableau, an image of companionship and peace, while the rhythmic sound of waves gliding onto the shore provided a soothing melody that enhanced the calm ambiance surrounding them. Each wave rolled in with a soft sigh, retreating as if to cradle the sand before drawing back into the endless depths of the ocean.

As Avyaan lifted his gaze skyward, he found himself captivated by the radiant moon, suspended high above like a silvery beacon guiding lost souls home. Its ethereal light bathed the landscape in a dreamlike glow, transforming the world around him into a fantastical realm bathed in magic. The moon's brilliance shimmered upon the water's surface, creating glistening pathways that seemed to beckon him toward the distant horizon, inviting him into the mysteries that lay beyond.

With a deep, contented sigh that resonated in his very core, Avyaan reached for his beloved, well-worn notebook—it's cover weathered, adorned with creases and scuffs that told tales of adventures that had shaped him over the years. He opened the notebook, revealing pages brimming with words and sketches, each a fragment of his life's journey filled with imagination and discovery. Inspired by the breathtaking beauty enveloping him and the tender bond of loyalty beside him, he felt a surge of creativity bubbling to the surface.

His pen glided across the pages like a dancer in perfect harmony with the rhythm of the night, as he composed a heartfelt poem dedicated to his beloved. The words flowed effortlessly, each line an ode to his unwavering love and longing, echoing through the stillness of the night. The verses intertwined seamlessly with the timeless lullaby of the crashing waves, creating a symphony of emotions that captured the essence of the moment and expressed the profound depth of his feelings under the watchful gaze of the luminous moon.

"The Sun was shining today, but it's not my sunshine,

The moon was lit today, but it was a black night,

The garden is big enough but without any flowers,

I dug this hole well enough, yet without any diamonds,

All this chaos is to have peace, but the truth is,

It's right there in your arms and now I understand it."

Avyaan sat in the soothing embrace of his dimly lit room, the atmosphere thick with an air of melancholy. His cherished book, well-worn and frayed at the edges, lay gently positioned on the aged wooden table beside him, each crease and mark telling tales of countless reads. Tears shimmered in his eyes, catching the soft glow of the nearby lamp like dew drops glistening on early morning grass. The weight of his swirling emotions pressed heavily upon his heart, a tangible ache that he could hardly bear. Yet, almost instinctively, his gaze drifted toward the radiant moon, which hung majestically in the velvety night sky. Its ethereal silvery light bathed his features, creating an almost dreamlike aura around him, offering a momentary escape from his turmoil. As the fringes of slumber began to pull him into their embrace, his thoughts delicately danced around Saanvi, her serene visage vividly etched in his mind. Her image brought a sense of peace, a flicker of comfort amidst the chaos engulfing his heart.

The dawn broke with an array of sounds drifting from outside—a gentle rustle of leaves, the cheerful chirping of birds—yet Avyaan was abruptly roused from his dreamy haze by Buddy, his loyal dog, who was barking with an urgency that cut through the tranquil morning air. Each sharp yip seemed to slice through the remaining fragments of sleep, and as he opened his eyes, he sensed Buddy's palpable excitement radiating from his every movement.

"What is it, boy? Where are you leading me?" he murmured groggily, a rush of curiosity igniting within him as he swung his legs off the bed and landed on the cool wooden floor. Following Buddy's enthusiastic lead, he followed the dog outside, feeling the refreshingly crisp morning air brush against his skin.

Their journey unfolded over three demanding hours, weaving through dense underbrush and climbing over rugged, weathered rocks that jutted from the earth like ancient sentinels. Each step brought him deeper into the embrace of nature, with birds singing overhead and the occasional rustle of a small creature darting through the undergrowth. Finally, they arrived at the mouth of a cave, its entrance narrow and somewhat foreboding. Shadows clung to the edges, whispering secrets of the unknown, and Avyaan felt a thrill of trepidation prick at the back of his mind. He hesitated for a moment, his heart pounding loudly in his chest, then he steeled his resolve and ventured inside. Instantly, a chill swept over him, causing his skin to prickle as the temperature dipped dramatically. The enveloping darkness pressed against him, heavy and suffocating, as he fumbled in his pocket for a flare. Striking it against the rough surface of the cave, a bright, flickering flame erupted to life, illuminating the cavern in a ghostly glow. The sudden burst of light startled a horde of bats, which took flight, fluttering wildly around him like a swirling tempest. Avyaan and Buddy instinctively recoiled, their hearts racing until the chaos finally settled into silence.

Once the eerie calm returned, Avyaan summoned the courage to push deeper into the cave, the flare casting dramatic shadows on the jagged walls around him. Each cautious step felt momentous as he explored the cavern, his heart racing with the thrill of the unknown. He combed through the shadows meticulously, searching for any glimmer of hidden treasure or signs of something extraordinary lying in wait. However, after an exhaustive exploration, their efforts yielded nothing more than echoes reverberating off the damp, rocky walls, merging with the thick silence that hung heavy in the air.

As daylight surrendered to dusk, the sun dipping below the horizon and surrendering the sky to a breathtaking palette of fiery oranges and deep purples, an unsettling feeling settled deep within Avyaan's core. The thought of retracing their steps back to camp, where the uncertainties and lurking thoughts of the night awaited, loomed heavily in his mind like an impending storm. Resolute in his decision, and despite the chill creeping into his bones, he chose to remain in the cave for the night. He was convinced that the stillness and enveloping darkness might cradle something yet undiscovered, something that could transform his restless feelings.

With renewed determination, they ventured deeper into the cave once more, a heady blend of adventure and trepidation wrapping around him like an inescapable shroud. They pressed on, navigating the intricate pathways until, all at once, a brilliant beam of moonlight sliced through a narrow crevice in the ceiling. The silvery glow pierced the oppressive shadows, illuminating the cavern in a breathtaking radiance that felt almost sacred. Intrigued, Avyaan approached cautiously, his heart pounding with a mixture of exhilaration and reverence. With tentative fingers, he tapped against the illuminated section of the wall, and an intriguing hollow reverberation echoed back to him, teasing the tantalizing prospect of a concealed space lurking just beyond the unyielding surface, promising the possibility of discovery the deeper they dared to venture.

Chapter 7:
An Impossible Task

After the darkest night, comes the

brightest morning,

When the cold left, spring showed

up,

When the storm ends, the clear sky

tells

How dynamic the World is...

Avyaan grabbed a big rock and threw it at the wall. The wall quickly shattered, revealing the treasure of the great Pirate.

The place was filled with corpses and treasure, indicating that he was not the first one to search for it. Avyaan quickly started collecting as much treasure as he could.

When he turned around, he saw a lot of spirits blocking the entrance of the cave. They screamed,

"This treasure is cursed! This place is cursed! You are now cursed! You are taking somebody's most valuable thing, now you have to sacrifice yours!" and then disappeared.

Avyaan's heart thundered in his chest, each beat echoing the whirlwind of disbelief and exhilaration that engulfed him as he absorbed the extraordinary reality of his astounding discovery. Before him lay an astonishing trove of treasure, each piece glistening brilliantly in the sun's resplendent rays, casting a kaleidoscope of reflections that danced playfully across the warm, earthy ground. The scene unfolded like a vivid dream, a stark contrast to the modest life he had known, which now felt like a distant memory. As he turned to make his way back to the campsite, a sensation of weightlessness enveloped him, as if he were floating just above the ground, his every step infused with dreams of newfound wealth and a kaleidoscope of opportunities that twirled tantalizingly through his mind.

He envisioned a life transformed, rich with the promise of prosperity and peace—one where he and his scruffy yet spirited dog could finally emerge from the oppressive shadows of hardship into a sun-drenched future brimming with possibilities. The thought of endless food, a cozy home, and the thrill of shared escapades with his faithful companion filled him with an intoxicating joy he had never before experienced.

As dawn broke, it unfurled like a breathtaking symphony of light. Soft hues of pink and gold spilled across the horizon, washing over the landscape and casting the world in a new, enchanting glow. Avyaan sprang into action, gathering the few essentials he would need for their departure; his well-worn backpack, a small pot for cooking, and a handful of provisions. Yet, despite the tangible preparations, his thoughts soared free, drifting toward memories of home—the warmth of laughter, the scent of familiar spices, and the sweetness of reconnecting with Saanvi. His heart swelled with yearning at the thought of her radiant smile, a beacon of hope that shone brighter than the glistening gold coins he had unearthed.

His loyal dog, a steadfast companion through life's upheavals, darted around him in joyous anticipation, its tail wagging energetically like a banner of exuberance that encapsulated their shared excitement for the journey ahead. Avyaan laughed, a genuine burst of joy spilling from him, momentarily washing away memories of past struggles as he envisioned their brilliant future together, full of laughter and adventures.

Upon returning to his village, the sight that greeted him was nothing short of extraordinary. A chorus of gasps intertwined with murmurs of disbelief as townsfolk gathered, their faces alight with wonder and eyes wide in astonishment. They gazed in awe at the gleaming treasure he had bravely unearthed, the golden coins catching the sunlight and casting a warm glow upon their faces. News of his staggering discovery rippled through the community like a mighty river, igniting a fervor that surged through the kingdom, binding hearts together in shared amazement and hope.

His heart raced, thrumming with a cocktail of exhilaration and dread as he envisioned the moment he would finally reunite with Saanvi. Each powerful stride sent adrenaline coursing through his veins as he sprinted toward her home, a charming sanctuary nestled gracefully atop the neighboring hill. However, as he drew closer, an unsettling silence draped itself over the quaint domicile, an oppressive stillness that constricted around his heart like a vice. A gnawing dread coiled tightly in his stomach, its grip only tightening when his gaze fell upon a letter propped conspicuously against the intricately carved door—a stark contrast against the inviting facade. The letter bore the Nawab's regal seal, an emblem he recognized all too well, and it sent a ripple of unease coursing through his body.

With trembling fingers, Avyaan tore the letter open, the paper crackling as he unfolded it. His eyes raced over the elegantly scripted words, each line weighted with an ominous significance that set his nerves alight. The note began with a facade of congratulations, but a sinister undercurrent wove through the words, sending icy chills skittering down his spine. The Nawab's message hinted at a daunting task, one that would not only dictate the course of Avyaan's own life but would irrevocably entwine Saanvi's fate with his own. The revelation that the true treasure he sought lay firmly in Nawab's grasp hit him like a sledgehammer, shaking him to the core and igniting a spark of dread deep within.

As night descended like an inky shroud, the stars twinkled overhead, distant gems scattered across an expansive black velvet canopy, casting a mesmerizing glow around him. A grim realization settled heavily upon Avyaan's shoulders; the curse he had dismissed as mere folklore now loomed ominously over him, casting a dark shadow that threatened to engulf his very soul. Anguish bubbled within him, intertwined with a fierce determination that forged an unbreakable resolve. He meticulously gathered his belongings, his loyal dog watching silently, eyes shining with unwavering devotion and a palpable eagerness to embark on this perilous journey by his side.

"I could never leave you behind, my faithful companion," Avyaan murmured softly, lifting his beloved dog onto the back of his sturdy horse with gentle care. The animal responded with an encouraging bark, the sound echoing through the night as if calling forth their shared courage for the challenges that lay ahead.

As dawn painted the horizon with soft, golden light, Avyaan found himself standing before the imposing castle of the Nawab. It towered grandly, its colossal walls casting long, intimidating shadows that stretched like the haunting fingers of the night. The air was thick with tension as he approached the entrance, where a door guard stood resolutely. Clad in ornate armor that glimmered in the early light, he bore an expression that was as stern and unyielding as a mountain.

Avyaan's determination solidified in the face of pressure. Clenching the royal order letter crumpled in his pocket, he felt a flicker of hope igniting within him. After presenting the letter with a grit born from desperation, the guard reluctantly granted him entry, leading him into a lavishly adorned chamber replete with opulence that spoke of wealth and power. The Nawab awaited, reclining with an air of calculated grace, his sharp eyes narrowing as they assessed Avyaan, an unexpected hint of surprise flickering within their depths.

"I did not expect to see you so soon," the Nawab remarked, his voice a blend of intrigue and suspicion, carefully molded into a mask of authority that belied his true intentions.

"Your Majesty! Where is Saanvi? I must see her," Avyaan implored, desperation weaving through every syllable. Each word felt heavy and choking in his throat; disbelief gnawed at him—how could he be separated from the girl he cherished so dearly?

"Not now, Avyaan! We have urgent matters to address." The Nawab's voice dropped to a low, menacing tone, emphasizing the finality of his words. *"Hidden somewhere within this castle lies a treasure of significant value. If you can uncover it, I shall release your beloved."*

"But this is unjust," Avyaan protested, feeling the crushing weight of his dire predicament pressing down upon him, threatening to drag him into an abyss of despair.

"Life does not always conform to notions of justice, treasure hunter," the Nawab replied coolly, his expression hardening beneath the glint of his royal garb. *"You have one month*

to find what is hidden. If you fail, I shall spare you the fate that befell the others, but be warned—your girl will suffer the consequences," he declared, his voice resonating with a chilling finality.

"You are dismissed!" The proclamation echoed ominously through the chamber, leaving Avyaan with no choice but to prepare for the daunting challenge ahead, the stakes now unmistakably and dangerously high.

Over the course of the next 26 days, Avyaan embarked on an exhaustive and tumultuous journey, his spirit igniting into a relentless engine driven by the tantalizing prospect of another world—one where an elusive treasure shimmered like a mirage, igniting his imagination with vivid dreams intricately woven from threads of adventure. Each new day unfolded seamlessly into the next, much like the turning pages of a well-worn, dog-eared novel, cradled by the whispers of tales yet to be told. However, the once-bright flame of his enthusiasm began to flicker, dimming beneath the heavy weight of frustration and a creeping despondency as his relentless quest yielded no tangible rewards. The unyielding pursuit gnawed at his very soul, wrapping shadows of doubt tightly around his every thought, and transforming his once-lofty aspirations into burdens too heavy to bear.

One fateful afternoon, as he ambled past Radha's room, an unusual incident suddenly seized his attention with an electric charge, shattering the routine of his weary heart. His loyal dog, a steadfast companion endowed with instincts sharper than Avyaan's own, erupted into a tempest of agitation. The dog barked furiously at the firmly shut door, straining against an invisible barrier—as if sensing an unseen presence lurking just beyond the threshold. Avyaan's mind raced with memories of the cautionary tales spun by a nearby soldier, whose unsettling anecdotes of bizarre occurrences in that very room had woven themselves into the fabric of local lore—whispers of mysterious sounds echoing through the silence, and objects shifting as if animated by spectral hands. Though the soldier's words hung in the air like a chilling shroud of foreboding, Avyaan brushed them aside as mere superstition, rationalizing that the uproar was likely nothing more than a wayward rodent scurrying about, searching for refuge.

Spurred by a surge of curiosity and perhaps a dash of reckless abandon, he summoned his courage and pushed open the door, stepping into the darkened space that exuded an oppressive aura of neglect. The air was thick and heavy, laden with dust that danced in faint beams of light filtering through the grimy window, and every breath was imbued with a musty scent reminiscent of long-forgotten memories, whispering that this room had been left to the ravages of time. Avyaan took a moment to survey the surroundings; his eyes adjusted slowly to the dimness, revealing several partially burnt crimson candles scattered haphazardly across a weathered table. Their waxy remains told haunting tales of bygone moments when flickers of light had dared to pierce through the shadows of this gloomy sanctuary. Driven by an insatiable determination to uncover potential clues lurking in the shadows, he pressed onward, exploring the stifling gloom with hesitant, deliberate steps.

As his hands sifted through the disarray, his fingers brushed against something coarse and familiar—a weathered diary, its cracked leather cover whispering secrets of age and forgotten tales. Intrigued, he delicately flipped through the fragile pages, and to his astonishment, he discovered that the diary belonged to a woman named Radha. Her final entry captivated him, revealing an intricate dance of apprehension interwoven with a flutter of anticipation regarding an impending meeting with a man named Vishnu. In the delicate, flowing script, she conjured vivid imagery of her emotions—expressing the palpable fear of being discovered, the agonizing pang of indecision gnawing at her as she fretted over which attire would best suit this momentous occasion, each word a testament to her hopes and fears that resonated deep within Avyaan's heart.

Just as the weight of her words began to envelop him in a contemplative haze, a sudden and thunderous crash shattered the silence, tearing through the heavy atmosphere like a lightning bolt. A chandelier, seemingly suspended in midair like some spectral apparition, plummeted to the ground with a bone-rattling shatter, sending shards of glass scattering across the room like glistening raindrops in the wake of a storm. A rush of adrenaline surged through Avyaan; his senses sharpened instantaneously in the face of this unforeseen danger. Glancing toward the window, he caught a fleeting glimpse of a dark shadow darting past the glass, triggering an instinctual retreat from the unsettling ambiance that clung to the room like a damp fog, suffocating his curiosity.

That evening, in a desperate search for solace, Avyaan found himself by the serene riverbank as twilight enveloped the world in dusky hues. The gentle lapping of the water against the shore provided a stark contrast to the tumult raging within his heart, serving both as a balm for his soul and a source of torment. Overwhelmed with emotion, he sank to the earth, the cool grass beneath him grounding him as his loyal dog curled up in his lap, offering silent comfort and companionship in his moment of despair. His thoughts were consumed with images of Saanvi—each one more haunting than the last—how could he ever hope to rescue her from whatever peril had ensnared her?

In the midst of his sorrow, a flicker of movement on the opposite riverbank drew his weary gaze. There, standing against the dusky backdrop like a ghostly apparition, was a woman clad in a striking crimson dress. The vibrant fabric shimmered defiantly against the encroaching darkness as if she were a beacon of hope amidst the all-consuming despair that had enveloped him. His dog, ever vigilant, raised its voice, barking insistently as if recognizing the significance of her presence. The sight of this mysterious figure deepened the intrigue of the unfolding mystery, leaving Avyaan torn between the agonizing weight of his grief and the tantalizing possibility of answers that beckoned from the shadows ahead, urging him to step back into the light of hope that had begun to flicker in his heart.

Chapter 8: Revelation of an Unfinished Story

Let the particle scattering guide their way,

Where they belong, they have done enough hustle,

Now all they deserve is to rest in peace.

Avyaan approached the woman with meticulous, cautious steps, his heart thrumming wildly in sync with the suspenseful tension that enveloped the air around them. His curiosity ignited like a firecracker as he observed the unmistakable tear stains that adorned her cheeks, shimmering softly like dewdrops captured in the fading light of the setting sun. Her once-vibrant eyes, once reminiscent of clear summer skies, now carried the weight of sorrow, shadowed and dulled, as if clouded by an impending storm of despair. A sense of urgency compelled him to speak, but just as he gathered his thoughts, an unrestrained dog burst past him. Its frantic barking sliced through the silence like a symphony caught in disarray, chasing after an elusive specter that danced on the horizon. Yet, despite this sudden chaos, Avyaan's unwavering desire to grasp the depths of her grief pulled him forward, drowning out the din of commotion that threatened to engulf them.

"What's troubling you?" he asked gently, his voice steady yet imbued with genuine concern, as though extending a fragile bridge between their worlds, which lay heavy with unspoken burdens.

At the sound of his voice, the woman hesitated, her sobs hitching painfully in her throat as she gasped for air, trying to compose herself. A haunting expression twisted her features as she began to turn away from him, her gaze narrowing on the gargantuan castle that loomed ominously against the backdrop of the twilit sky, its ancient, jagged spires reaching upward like spectral fingers clawing desperately at the fading light. Compelled by an instinctive pull, Avyaan followed the trajectory of her gaze, a wave of unsettling familiarity crashing over him as the realization struck deep; they were both drawn toward the very chamber he had fled mere hours before—a sanctuary he had yearned to escape.

Arriving at the imposing, heavy oak door, the woman glided inside with ethereal grace, her presence seemingly weightless as if the burdens of her grief had become momentarily suspended in the thickening haze of twilight. Avyaan hesitated, an overwhelming blend of intrigue and dread churning within him, yet an invisible force tugged at him, inviting him deeper into the unknown. He finally crossed the threshold, and as the ponderous door swung shut with a disconcerting finality, the deep thud echoed through the vast chamber like a harbinger of doom. A metallic click sounded as the door locked behind him, and a flood of panic surged through his veins, igniting his heart into a chaotic drumbeat. To his astonishment, the woman had vanished, leaving him alone in the dimly lit sanctuary that morphed quickly from a refuge to a suffocating prison.

As his eyes adjusted to the muted, flickering light, they unveiled a scene that sent a chill racing through him: partially burned candles sputtered to life, their flames dancing erratically as if summoned by an unseen specter. The dim glow cast elongated, quivering shadows that slinked across the bloodstained walls, deep crimson streaks grotesquely contrasting with the somber, gray hue of the ancient stone. A wave of cold panic surged within him as his gaze snapped to the walls, where desperate scrawls etched in a hurried hand begged for aid. The words twisted and writhed with urgency, starkly marked into the stone as if inscribed by fingers clawing for release: *"Please, help me!"* This haunting plea echoed in his mind, intertwining with the lingering remnants of the woman's anguished cries and muffled sobs that resonated hauntingly in the heavy silence.

Just as a bone-chilling shiver slithered down his spine, the sharp, resolute sound of knocking erupted from a nearby cabinet, its rhythm deliberate and unnerving. The sudden noise froze him in place, each resounding knock amplifying his unease and dragging him deeper into the unsettling depths of the unknown. It was as if the very walls around him were alive, pulsating with unspeakable secrets, beckoning him to uncover the buried truths hidden within their haunting shadows. Avyaan was consumed by the fear of his death, despite that he pulled the door of the cabinet and found the corpse of Radha. Her half-skeletonized body was looking straight into his soul desperately asking him to help her.

He saw a ring on one of the fingers of the corpse he took it out from it. When he drew the object from its sheath, the flickering candles in the room extinguished, the atmosphere grew heavy, and a woman materialized before Avyaan. Fierce anger blazed in her red eyes as she unleashed a piercing scream, propelling him through the window and into the night, shattering glass in his wake. After a harrowing fall from the second floor of an old, decrepit building,

Avyaan lay on the cold ground, disoriented and in excruciating pain. The world around him had blurred, but the sharp pain in his leg and the heaviness of his bruised body were painfully clear. In that moment of vulnerability, his loyal dog, a scruffy yet brave companion named Max, sensed his distress. Without hesitation, Max raced off, barking urgently to attract the attention of nearby soldiers who were patrolling the area.

The soldiers, alerted by the frantic barks, swiftly made their way to Avyaan's side. They carefully lifted him and transported him to a neighboring village, where a small but bustling clinic awaited. A kind-hearted medic tended to his injuries, wrapping his bruised leg with care and advising him to take at least five days of bed rest to aid in his recovery. However, deep inside him, anxiety churned as thoughts of Saanvi's peril flooded his mind. Ignoring the pain and medical advice, Avyaan resolved to set off for the castle that very night, determined to bring Saanvi back to safety, and he knew he couldn't bear to leave Max behind.

As darkness fell, they ventured into the dense forest that surrounded the village, the moonlight casting eerie shadows around them. Halfway through their journey, a chilling howl echoed through the trees—suddenly, a menacing pack of wolves emerged from the underbrush, hunger shining in their eyes. Avyaan felt his heart race as the wolves encircled them, their growls sending a shiver down his spine. With his injuries weighing him down and his strength dwindling, he realized he'd have no chance of fending them off alone. In a moment of desperation, he called out for help, his voice trembling with fear.

To his immense relief, from the shadows stepped a mysterious figure, cloaked and commanding. Without a word, the enigmatic man brandished a stout staff, rallying against the wolves with swift, precise movements. The wolves, sensing the powerful presence of their adversary, retreated into the darkened woods, leaving Avyaan and Max unharmed, albeit shaken.

The stranger insisted they seek refuge in his nearby hut, a humble dwelling nestled between the trees. Once inside, the man took meticulous care of their injuries, applying herbal remedies and wrapping bandages around Avyaan's bruises with skilled hands. Avyaan felt a strange sense of comfort in this man's presence, though his origins were shrouded in mystery.

As dawn broke, the first light filtering through the cracks of the hut's wooden walls, Avyaan rushed to prepare for departure. However, the man urged him to stay a little longer and share breakfast. Reluctantly agreeing, Avyaan sat at a rustic wooden table, where they broke bread together. During the meal, the man's sharp gaze fell upon a glinting ring on Avyaan's finger. Curiosity sparked in his eyes, and he asked about the ring's origins.

With a sigh, Avyaan recounted the tale of how he had unearthed the ring while exploring the castle, believing it to be a key to the treasure hidden within. As he spoke, he couldn't help but wonder if the ring held greater significance and what role it might play in the quest that still lay ahead for him and Saanvi.

The man's eyes widened in shock as he quickly recognized the ring resting delicately in Avyaan's outstretched palm. A wave of conflicting emotions surged through him, crashing over the shores of his composure.

"Where is that woman?" he demanded, his voice a blend of anger and concern that deepened with each word.

"Did you steal this from her? This ring was a precious gift I gave to my wife!" The tremor in his voice betrayed the urgency of his feelings, echoing through the tense silence that enveloped them.

As Avyaan steadied himself, he inhaled deeply, attempting to gather the fragmented threads of his courage. He began to recount the harrowing events that had transpired within the confines of Radha's room. He spoke of the oppressive, eerie ambiance that had wrapped around him like a heavy cloak, the unsettling chill that prickled at his skin, and the ghostly presence that had lingered long after Radha's departure. As his words flowed, Vishnu's face drained of color, his expression morphing into one of mounting horror. A tempest of emotions flickered in his eyes, painting a vivid picture of disbelief and dread. Every syllable seemed to constrict around him, bearing down with an unrelenting weight that made him feel as though he were submerged in an icy abyss.

Overwhelmed by the gravity of the tale, Vishnu hesitated, his internal battle evident in the way his brow furrowed and his body tensed. He shook his head slowly, the movement heavy with reluctance, and the tension in his shoulders hinted at an instinctive desire to retreat from the chilling notion before him.

"I can't go with you," he finally whispered his voice a mere breath, quivering with unspoken fears. The idea of stepping into that haunted space filled him with an overwhelming sense of dread, a primal urge to recoil from the dark, foreboding journey that lay ahead.

"I have read some of the letters where she was excited & nervous to meet you. How did

*she end up with that tragic demise? Why didn't you save her? "*Avyaan asked.

"I tried to save her by putting my own life on the line, during that I lost a friend too. But when I entered the room I found no one, Nawab's soldiers were on my back already which forced me to jump out of the window. Everybody thought I was eaten by the crocodiles, but luckily I managed to escape. From that day till now I was trying to find her but I didn't get any clue. I thought she ran away or the soldiers might have taken her into custody but now I feel so hopeless and shattered." Vishnu cries.

Avyaan appealed to Vishnu's sense of compassion stating,

"If you ever cared for her, don't you believe she deserves a proper farewell? The state in which I found her body was truly horrific. She deserves a peaceful departure from this world, and only you can provide that for her."

Vishnu realized that he was echoing his own sentiments through Avyaan's words and ultimately agreed to join him.

Avyaan entrusted the ring to Vishnu, and they made plans to visit Radha's room at night when it was deserted.

Chapter 9:
The Final Goodbye

Destiny is already written,

We are just a puppet in this stage of

the world & Living in this

simulation...

As the last tendrils of daylight surrendered to a sprawling crimson horizon, the sky transformed into a canvas of vibrant orange and deep purple hues, Avyaan and Vishnu moved with palpable urgency, their hearts racing as they prepared for the treacherous journey that lay ahead. Their faithful companion, a scruffy little terrier with a tousled coat that mirrored the wildness of his spirit, seemed to sense the weight of the moment. With instinctive awareness, he barked anxiously, his wide, dark eyes brimming with concern, a silent plea for his beloved friends not to brave the unknown dangers alone.

Avyaan knelt on the cool, damp ground, his expression softening as he scooped the dog into his arms. The warmth radiating from the furry creature provided a brief moment of solace amid the tense atmosphere that thickened around them like an impending storm. His voice quivered with a blend of determination and tenderness as he whispered, *"I won't abandon you this time. You've sacrificed so much for me before, but I promise, I'll return soon."* Each word resonated with sincerity, lingering in the crisp evening air while the dog gazed up at him, his tail wagging faintly, seemingly understanding the profound weight of the vow being made.

In the distance, the ancient castle loomed against the backdrop of the dusky sky, its silhouette resembling a foreboding specter cloaked in dense mist that swirled ominously around its weathered, crumbling stone walls. Once a gleaming emblem of splendor, it now exuded an aura of malevolence that sent shivers down Vishnu's spine. His heart raced violently, a tempest of fear coursing through him like electric currents, cold sweat trickling down his spine. Inner turmoil gripped him like an unyielding iron shackle, each instinct screaming warnings of the dangers that awaited; yet, he steeled himself, inhaling deeply before taking a hesitant yet resolute step toward the ominous fortress.

A sudden, powerful gust of wind rushed through the clearing, sending leaves into a chaotic dance while scattering the ominous clouds overhead as if the castle itself had sensed their approach, its presence both inviting and intimidating. The sound of their footsteps was nearly swallowed by the howling wind, a haunting symphony urging them onward as they navigated through a narrow, concealed passage long hidden from the watchful eyes of the Nawab's soldiers. A fierce sense of urgency ignited within their hearts, propelling them relentlessly toward Radha's chamber, the very reason for their audacious incursion into this shadowy realm.

As they finally approached the threshold of the chamber, an unsettling creak cut through the heavy silence, and the colossal door swung open with an eerie fluidity, as if summoned by an unseen force. Vishnu felt a strange, irresistible pull drawing him inside, a magnetic call that resonated with a profound, unspoken yearning deep within his soul. Avyaan positioned himself against the cold, damp stone wall in a shadowy corner, striving to remain unseen, and summoned his courage, calling out, *"Radha! I've come to rescue you! Reveal yourself!"*

A profound silence draped itself over the room, enveloping them in a heavy, oppressive shroud. The air felt thick with anticipation, almost tangible with tension. Heart racing and throat parched, Vishnu repeated her name, desperation seeping into his voice as each syllable echoed hauntingly in the cavernous space. Just then, in response to his heartfelt plea, a single candle flickered to life on a nearby pedestal, the flame dancing perilously in the stillness, casting a warm yet eerie glow that painted the chamber in hues of gold, mingled with deep shadows.

As the candlelight grew brighter, it illuminated a spectral figure—Radha's apparition—her presence a luminous specter shimmering softly in the warm light. Clad in the exquisite beige gown she had worn during their last cherished encounter, her silhouette exuded an unsettling blend of beauty and sorrow, serving as a poignant reminder of the joy they had once shared. Radha's intense gaze locked onto Vishnu's, her eyes flooded with an ocean of sorrow.

"Vishnu, you're late! Why did you not come to save me?" Tears cascaded down her translucent cheeks, falling like delicate raindrops onto the cold stone floor, echoing with the profound sadness that had taken root deep within her heart. The anguish in her voice reverberated through the chamber, striking a poignant chord within Vishnu's very soul, and igniting an unquenchable determination to rescue her from the clutches of despair.

"I trusted you, and you betrayed me, fleeing like a coward!" she exclaimed, consumed by anguish.

She grabbed Vishnu's neck and threw him up to the ceiling. The ring fell out of Vishnu's pocket and dropped on the floor in front of Radha. She looked at the ring, and her anger vanished. Vishnu said,

"Radha! I came to rescue you, but when I entered the room, you were nowhere to be found. The enemies were closing in on me, so I had to make a split-second decision and jump out of the window. I thought you had already fled the castle. I've been tirelessly searching for you for the past six months," Vishnu confessed with tears in his eyes.

"I'm here to take you out of this place," he added.

Radha gazed deep into his eyes and inquired, *"Do you still have feelings for me?"*

Vishnu responded, *"Yes, Radha. I've loved you from the moment I first laid eyes on you, when you were just 13 years old, picking fruits in the orchards with your mother near the castle. I used to watch you while training for the army recruitment."*

"Will you come with me?" Radha asked him.

Vishnu didn't hesitate for another second and agreed.

Avyaan, who was in the corner, watching everything. He interrupted them and asked, *"Vishnu! Think again. Do you know what you are doing?"*

Vishnu turned around and said, *"The day I was separated from Radha, I felt like a flower that had been plucked from the ground. I started to feel like I had begun to wither. I would rather die and be happy ever after with my love than live a lifeless life."*

Radha and Vishnu stepped towards each other. Vishnu pulled her close to him by her waist. He leaned her down in his arms and kissed her lips.

The room was dimly lit by flickering candles, casting eerie shadows on the walls. Suddenly, as the last candle vanished,

Vishnu's soul seemed to depart from his body, causing him to collapse to the ground.

In a quiet, hidden corner of the house, the window in Radha's room let out a soft, haunting creak as it mysteriously slid open, as though summoned by an invisible force. Radha and Vishnu felt an enchanting pull, an inexplicable attraction that compelled them to rise from the floor, their feet slowly lifting off the ground as they began to ascend into the vast, star-studded night sky. The air surrounding them shimmered with an ethereal glow, wrapping them in a veil of enigma that whispered the ancient secrets of the universe.

Meanwhile, beneath the sprawling expanse of twinkling stars, Avyaan positioned himself carefully on the soft grass, gazing upward with rapt attention. He watched Chukoor, who perched eagerly on a sturdy branch of the venerable oak tree, his eyes glinting with excitement. As he strained to glimpse the moon making its grand entrance from behind the thick curtain of clouds, his heart raced, anticipation coursing through him. Suddenly, in an explosion of light, the night transformed as the moon broke free, casting a luminous glow that radiated like a precious pearl. The gentle light spilled across the landscape, illuminating everything around it and weaving a tapestry of enchanting shadows that enhanced the natural beauty of the scene, turning the familiar into something magical.

Caught in the moment of magic, Chukoor felt an irresistible surge of exhilaration. Without a second thought, he leaped from the branch, defying gravity for an exhilarating heartbeat as he soared into the night sky, arms outstretched as if he were trying to grasp the glowing orb itself. The moonbeams danced around him, wrapping him in a celestial embrace as he ascended, leaving behind the earthly bounds that had kept him grounded.

Later, as the night deepened, Avyaan performed solemn funeral rites for both Vishnu and Radha on the tranquil riverbank, the flickering flames of the funeral pyre casting an otherworldly glow on the mournful scene.

Chapter 10:
The Treasure

When we think it is all ending,

It is actually the beginning of

something new.

The impending deadline to uncover the long-lost treasure loomed over Avyaan like a dark storm cloud, casting an oppressive shadow that stretched across his every waking thought. Each passing moment felt akin to a relentless tide, pulling him deeper into a sea of anxiety, the pressure intensifying as the hours dwindled from hours to mere minutes. An anticipation gnawed at his insides, twisting his gut tightly, and suffocating him with the weight of uncertainty.

The Nawab, a formidable figure adorned in richly embellished garments that glimmered like a mirage under the faint castle lights, summoned Avyaan for an audience. His presence was commanding; he moved with an air of authority that resonated through the chamber. Piercing eyes, sharp like daggers and seemingly capable of unraveling secrets, scrutinized Avyaan as he entered. There was an impatient intensity in the Nawab's demeanor, and it was clear that he expected swift results.

"Have any valuable tidings emerged?" he demanded, his voice dripping with an undercurrent of menace that wrapped around Avyaan like a tightening noose. The words reverberated off the stone walls, amplifying the enormity of the moment. Avyaan felt the immense weight of the situation descends upon him like an oppressive shroud, stifling his breath. Mustering every ounce of

courage he could muster, he replied, *"Rest assured, my lord, the treasure will be revealed by dawn."* Even as he spoke, his heart thudded heavily in his chest, and a flicker of doubt ignited ominously in the deepest corners of his mind.

The Nawab's reaction was explosive, sending shockwaves of fear racing through the room. His face contorted into an expression of rage, and he unleashed a chilling ultimatum that hung in the air like thick smoke.

"Should you fail, my dear Avyaan, it will not only be you who suffer the consequences. Think carefully about your loved ones." Each word was laced with a cruel finality that sent a shiver down Avyaan's spine. With a dismissive wave that sliced through the tension, the Nawab sent Avyaan away, leaving him to navigate the hallowed, echoing halls of the castle—each step heavier than the last, weighed down by the

dreadful thought of the danger looming over his loved ones.

As the day unfolded into a cruel game of elusive time, each hour slipped away without yielding any clues about the treasure's hidden whereabouts. Avyaan wandered through the castle's maze-like corridors, the chill of the stone walls wrapping around him in a tight embrace, his footsteps echoing in the unnatural silence. Desperation gripped him as he scoured every nook and cranny of the castle, rummaging through dusty tomes whose spines cracked with age and forgotten artifacts that lay covered in neglect. Each lead turned cold, leaving him more disheartened and defeated, the pangs of futility pressing down upon him like a massive boulder, suffocating him beneath its weight.

Eventually, he sank beneath the gnarled, sprawling branches of a centuries-old tree, the bark rough against his skin, providing little comfort to the turmoil raging within. Consumed by frustration and helplessness, exhaustion enveloped him, and he drifted into a troubled slumber, tears of despair streaming down his cheeks like silent pleas, while the shadows of dark dreams loomed ever closer, whispering threats of failure.

In the dead of night, a hauntingly beautiful melody wafted through the still air, invading the recesses of his restless sleep with a mesmerizing allure. Curiosity and dread danced in his chest as he followed the ethereal music, its notes curling around him like a soft fog, drawing him ever closer. As he navigated through the dimly lit corridors, shadows flitted across the walls, and he stumbled upon a scene that seized his heart with fear—every guard, usually a vigilant sentinel, lay scattered across the floor like discarded leaves in the autumn wind, their bodies sprawled in eerie stillness. The castle's corridors, once bustling with life, now seemed shrouded in an ominous quiet, heightening the sense of dread that clung to him like a second skin.

With a renewed determination igniting his spirit like a blazing fire, he pressed onward through the darkened corridors, the haunting melody of a distant flute guiding his every step. Each note resonated within him, a symphony of hope and fear intertwining. Finally, he found himself standing before a formidable locked door, its heavy wooden frame looming over him like a sentinel of fate, an impenetrable barrier between him and his goal. The key—a glimmer of opportunity—was tightly gripped in the calloused hand of an unconscious soldier who lay just beyond his reach, a silent guardian of secrets.

Time slipped through his fingers like grains of sand, and with the utmost caution, he eased the key from the soldier's inert grasp. A rush of adrenaline surged through him, electrifying his veins as his heart raced in anticipation. He approached the door, his hand trembling slightly as he inserted the key into the lock. The door creaked open with a groan that echoed eerily, revealing a dimly lit chamber that spilled shadows across the stone floor.

Inside lay a scene that sent a whirlwind of both relief and dread coursing through his veins—a vision of Saanvi, standing there with a face streaked by tears, her expression a painful echo of her suffering. Without a moment's hesitation, Avyaan rushed to her side. He enveloped her in a protective embrace as if trying to shield her from the chaotic world outside. The weight of their separation melted away in that fleeting moment, and Saanvi, overwhelmed yet incredulous, expressed her astonishment at being reunited with him. Time seemed to suspend, and in that embrace, her arms tightened around him, their souls intertwining in the assurance that they were still together, still alive against all odds.

"We must escape," Avyaan urged, his voice steady and resolute, infused with an urgency that filled the air around them. He lifted her into his arms, every movement fueled by the fierce determination to break free. Together, they hurried toward the castle's grand entrance, his heart thundering wildly with the urgency of their flight. As they neared the exit, a flicker of movement caught his eye, and to his astonishment, he recognized a man and a woman standing together, hands intertwined—the embodiment of legends he had only heard of through whispered tales of

bravery. It was Vishnu and Radha, the renowned saviors whose bravery had been instrumental in Saanvi's rescue.

Their smiles radiated warmth and reassurance, a beacon of hope in their turbulent world, but before he could fully grasp their presence, they seemed to dissolve into the very air around them, leaving behind a lingering aura of awe and gratitude, a transient blessing that enveloped them both.

"Thank you," Avyaan whispered into the enveloping night, his heart swelling with appreciation for the miracle that had unfolded.

"Thank you?" Saanvi echoed, confusion etching a frown upon her delicate features as she looked up at him, searching his eyes for understanding.

"Nothing, let's go," he replied quickly, the urgency palpable in his voice as they took

their first, tentative steps toward freedom, the looming silhouette of the castle gradually fading into the vast darkness behind them.

Avyaan guided Saanvi to the rustic hut where he had once sought refuge with Vishnu. Here, they concealed themselves for several weeks, hiding in the humble sanctuary as Nawab's soldiers scoured the land in relentless pursuit of Avyaan, the handsome reward on his head casting a shadow over their every move. One fateful day, while gathering wood in the dense embrace of the forest, Avyaan was suddenly apprehended by a soldier, his world spinning into chaos as he was brought before the Nawab in the opulent, forbidding grand hall.

"So, you thought you could slip away so easily?" the Nawab sneered.

"I have discovered the treasure," Avyaan calmly responded.

"What! Where is it? Tell me this instant!" the Nawab demanded desperately.

A sudden crack echoed through the hall as a pillar collapsed, crushing the Nawab beneath it. Chaos erupted within the castle as the tension escalated. Avyaan seized a fleeting opportunity to escape, his heart pounding in his chest. With quick, decisive movements, he mounted his steed and beckoned for Saanvi to join him. Without hesitation, she climbed on behind him, her arms wrapping tightly around his waist as they galloped into the enveloping darkness of the night.

The moon hung high in the sky, casting a silvery glow that illuminated their path as they rode away from the towering castle in the distance. After what felt like an eternity, they arrived at his village, a place that now felt both familiar and foreign. It was there, amidst the rustic charm of thatched roofs and winding dirt paths, that Avyaan unveiled the secret he had risked so much to secure: a trove of glittering gems and ancient artifacts hidden within his saddlebag.

"We must leave at first light. This place is no longer safe for us," Avyaan declared, his voice steady but laced with urgency. Saanvi nodded in silent agreement, her eyes reflecting a mixture of excitement and apprehension.

Avyaan paused, his brow furrowed in contemplation. *"Saanvi, I have come to a profound realization,"* he began, the seriousness of his tone commanding her full attention.

"What is it, Avyaan?" she asked, curiosity piquing her interest as she studied his expression.

"The true treasure I have sought in this world is not the riches I have discovered," Avyaan confessed, his gaze softening. "I have been celebrated as a master hunter,

known for my prowess and skill, yet I failed to see that the real treasure has always been right beside me. Saanvi, that treasure is you." His heartfelt words hung in the air, and Saanvi felt a warm blush creep across her cheeks as she processed his confession. She stepped forward, her heart swelling with emotion, and embraced him tightly, feeling the sincerity of his feelings envelop them both.

With dawn fast approaching, Avyaan invited her to wander through their village one last time. He longed to savor the beauty of the place that had been his home, knowing this day would mark their final moments there. They strolled hand-in-hand to a tranquil lake nestled at the edge of the village, its surface reflecting the vibrant hues of the awakening sky.

As night transformed quietly into day, they spent hours sharing stories, laughter, and dreams for what lay ahead, their bond deepening with each passing moment. With the sun breaking the horizon, painting the sky in shades of orange and gold, Avyaan felt an overwhelming desire to commemorate their time together.

Reaching into his pocket, Avyaan retrieved a delicate necklace, crafted from shimmering silver and adorned with a single shimmering gemstone that mirrored the hues of the dawn. Gently, he placed it around Saanvi's neck, the cool metal resting against her skin.

"This is a token of my love for you, a reminder that even in the face of uncertainty, you are my greatest treasure," he murmured softly, his eyes locking onto hers with unwavering sincerity. Saanvi's heart fluttered, and in that moment, they both understood that their journey was only beginning, and their true adventure lay in the bond they shared.

They made ready to depart at daybreak to avoid detection, leaving their home engulfed in flames. When the villagers arrived, all they found were ashes, presuming Avyaan and Saanvi had perished.

Avyaan and Saanvi embarked on a transformative journey that marked a significant turning point in their lives. With a shared resolve, they began to shed the heavy burdens of their pasts—painful memories and regrets—and embraced new identities that perfectly echoed their aspirations for a brighter future filled with hope and possibility. Each dawn brought new opportunities and adventures, and they immersed themselves in this vibrant life, allowing their personalities to flourish as they uncovered the profound beauty of love woven into the fabric of their relationship.

Their commitment to each other blossomed beautifully, ultimately culminating in a breathtaking wedding ceremony that felt like a fairytale. The scene was set under a starlit sky, illuminated by the soft, twinkling glow of fairy lights strung above, creating a magical ambiance. Surrounded by a close-knit circle of friends and family—each of whom celebrated the vibrant, joyful versions of Avyaan and Saanvi that had emerged—laughter and joy intertwined with every heartfelt vow exchanged. Each promise they made was not only a declaration of love but also a commitment to navigating life's inevitable challenges together, hand in hand.

In the heart of their shared home, Avyaan and Saanvi cultivated an environment that radiated warmth and joy. Every corner of the house was a reflection of their love and partnership; the cozy living room boasted a collection of photographs capturing their adventures, laughter, and quiet moments together. Each image told a story, a cherished memory contributing to the tapestry of their life. In the quaint kitchen, they spent countless hours preparing meals side by side, transforming everyday ingredients into culinary delights, each dish infused with love and creativity. These shared moments became a testament to their partnership, fostering a deeper bond with every meal cooked and shared.

As the seasons shifted and the years seemed to slip by in the blink of an eye, Avyaan and Saanvi walked through life side by side, their hands intertwined, navigating both joyous peaks and heart-wrenching valleys with unwavering support for one another. Their love stood resilient, forged through shared dreams, laughter, and the occasional challenge that tested their resolve. They cherished every fleeting moment together, weaving a rich tapestry of memories that celebrated joy, resilience, and a legacy of happiness. Each experience they shared became a note in their love story—a testament to the enduring echo of their hearts, forever intertwined in love and companionship.